MAX & MO's
First Day at School

WITHDRAWN

For another set of best friends,
Max and Mia —P. L.

For George —B. F.

SIMON SPOTLIGHT
AN IMPRINT OF SIMON & SCHUSTER CHILDREN'S PUBLISHING DIVISION
1230 AVENUE OF THE AMERICAS, NEW YORK, NY 10020
TEXT COPYRIGHT © 2007 BY PATRICIA LAKIN
ILLUSTRATIONS COPYRIGHT © 2007 BY BRIAN FLOCA
ALL RIGHTS RESERVED, INCLUDING THE RIGHT OF REPRODUCTION IN
WHOLE OR IN PART IN ANY FORM.
READY-TO-READ IS A REGISTERED TRADEMARK OF
SIMON & SCHUSTER, INC.
SIMON SPOTLIGHT AND RELATED LOGO ARE REGISTERED
TRADEMARKS OF SIMON & SCHUSTER, INC.
DESIGNED BY LISA VEGA
THE TEXT OF THIS BOOK WAS SET IN CENTURY OLDSTYLE BT.
MANUFACTURED IN THE UNITED STATES OF AMERICA 0918 LAK
FIRST ALADDIN PAPERBACKS EDITION JUNE 2007
10
LIBRARY OF CONGRESS CATALOGING-IN-PUBLICATION DATA
LAKIN, PATRICIA, 1944–
MAX AND MO'S FIRST DAY AT SCHOOL / BY PATRICIA LAKIN ;
ILLUSTRATED BY BRIAN FLOCA.—1ST ALADDIN PAPERBACKS ED.
P. CM.—(READY-TO-READ)
SUMMARY: WHEN MAX AND MO, TWO CLASS HAMSTERS, RETURN TO
SCHOOL AND ARE PLACED IN THE ART ROOM, THEY USE SUPPLIES FOUND
THERE TO SPELL OUT THEIR NAMES FOR THE STUDENTS. INCLUDES
DIRECTIONS FOR MAKING A NAME TAG USING HOUSEHOLD ITEMS.
ISBN: 978-1-4169-2533-0 (PBK)
ISBN: 978-1-4169-2534-7 (LIBRARY)
[1. HANDICRAFT—FICTION. 2. HAMSTERS—FICTION.
3. SCHOOLS—FICTION.] I. FLOCA, BRIAN, ILL. II. TITLE.
PZ7.L1586MAX 2007
[E]—DC22
2006025871

MAX & MO's
First Day at School

By Patricia Lakin
Illustrated by Brian Floca

Ready-to-Read

Simon Spotlight
New York   London   Toronto   Sydney   New Delhi

Max and Mo
were best friends.
They lived in a cozy cage.

BING BANG BOING!

"We are moving!"
they cried.

"Where to?" said Max.

"Back to school,"
said Mo.
"It is our first day,"
said Max.

Mo read the sign.
"We are in the art room."

"New things to make,"
said Max.
"And new friends, too,"
said Mo.
They waited for
the big ones.

"Hello!" called out
Max and Mo.

"She called me Tummy,"
  said Mo.
"He called me Fluffy,"
  said Max.
"They do not know
  our names," they said.

"We need name tags!"
they said.

Max scratched his chin.
"How do we make them?"
Mo scratched his ears.
"We need to get out!"

The big ones left.
Max climbed on Mo.

Up and out
went Max.

Up and out
went Mo!

"This book tells us
what to do," said Mo.

They took the roll.
They wrapped it.
They taped it.

Mo wrote.

Max poured . . .

and rolled.

"That is my name,"
said Mo.
"That is my name,"
said Max.

"Help!" cried Max.
"It is rolling."

Mo read,
"Cut a straw in two.
Now tape."
"No more rolling,"
said Max and Mo.

"Oops!" they said.

"It needs to go in our cage!"

"How?" said Max.

"Lift up!" said Mo.

"Tilt up!"
"Climb up!"

"Tilt down!"

"Slide down!"

"Wheeee!"

They curled up
and waited for the big ones.
"Hello, Max and Mo,"
the big ones all said.

Want to make a name tag
for a "big one"?

Here is what you need:
1. A grown-up's help
2. An inside roll from paper
   towels
3. 1 piece of paper
4. Tape
5. Scissors
6. A straw
7. Glue
8. Seeds or rice
9. Paper punch (if you want to
   make a pencil holder)

Here is how:

1. WRAP

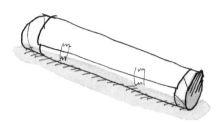

2. TAPE

MAX AND MO

3. WRITE

4. POUR

5. ROLL

6. CUT

7. TAPE

8. PUNCH

9. SLIP

10. DONE!